This is My Book

Name _____

Date _____

2002

ISBN 1-887327-20-7

JOHNNY TRACTOR AND FRIENDS

WORKING TOGETHER

A JOHN DEERE STORYBOOK FOR LITTLE FOLKS

From a Story by T.J. Cahill

Illustrated by Kirk Barron

The equipment shed was full of chatter that night. The different machines couldn't stop talking about how hard it was raining. "Have you ever heard it rain so hard?" said Danny Dozer to his friends, Luke Loader and Grady Grader.

"Not me," said Luke. "It is coming down in buckets as big as mine." "Well, I have" said Grady, "and that means tomorrow I will have to work extra hard to fix up all the roads."

"Can we help?" asked Luke. "Why, of course not," said Grady. "Everybody knows loaders are for digging. I need to level and smooth all the dirt back into place." "Danny can push dirt," Luke replied. "Can't he help?" "Why, of course not," Grady said, "he can't smooth the road like I can. Only I can do this job!"

Danny knew Grady liked to brag a little, so before there was an argument between his friends he told them to get a good night's sleep. Tomorrow would be a busy day.

The next day was sunny and bright, and the air was clean and fresh. The three friends were up early and on their way to Fowler Road. "I don't understand why you two have to come along," said Grady to Danny and Luke.

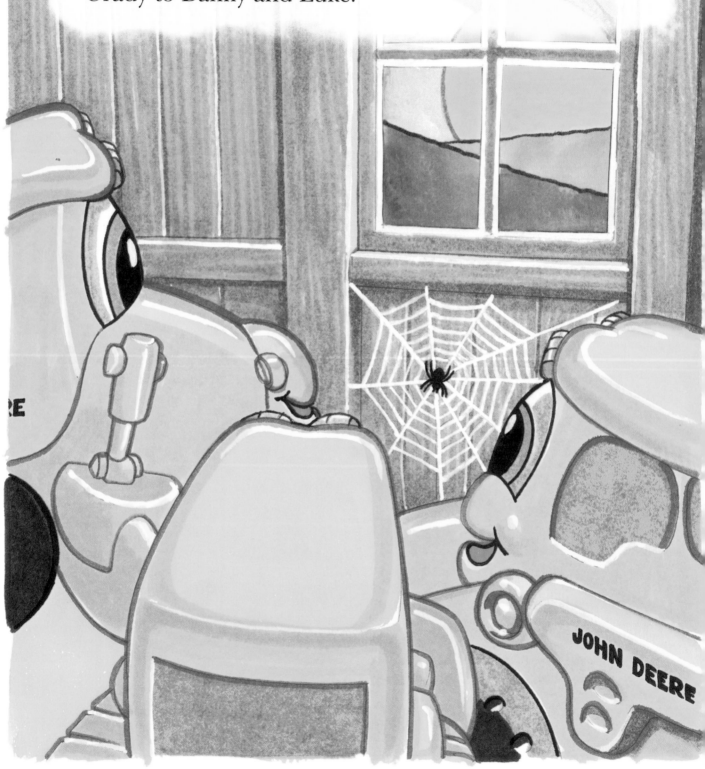

"We are just coming along to see what a good job you will do," said Danny.

Danny and Luke heard the boss tell the workers about a big washout on the road to the Fowler Farm and how everybody was needed to help fix it. But they did not tell Grady.

"Oh, my," said Grady when he saw the big hole in the road. "How can I fix this?" Danny and Luke watched as Grady looked at the road, knowing he could not fix it by himself.

"We can help!" said Danny and Luke. Grady knew he needed help from his friends, but was afraid to ask after what he told them the night before.

"Don't worry," said Danny. "We know this job is too big for just one of us." "We will help you," said Luke. Grady was embarrassed, but was glad his friends were there to help him. Then they went to work.

Luke Loader filled his big bucket with dirt and dumped it in the hole. Danny was busy pushing dirt to the hole and filling it in.

They worked and worked until the hole was filled. Grady watched how hard his friends worked to help him. He was proud they were his friends.

Finally, Grady was able to go to work and level and smooth the road to just like new.

The three friends looked at each other after the job was done. Grady said, "I will never brag again, and will always ask for help if I need it." Luke and Danny agreed.

On the way back to the shed that sunny afternoon, Danny said to his friends, "Isn't it a lot of fun *working together*?"